n Scowe

The
Mysterious
Greatwood

*Written and illustrated
by Michael Clark*

TEWIN ORCHARD

First published by Hamish Hamilton 1972
This first colour Tewin Orchard edition 2007

ISBN 978-0-9549508-1-1
Copyright © 1972 & 2007
text and illustrations Michael Clark
EAN 9780954950811

For Anna, Ben, Sarah and Susie

*Special thanks to Linda Jennings
who gave the book its first life in monochrome
and Emma Pitrakou for her design work
in this new edition*

Published by Tewin Orchard
1 Upper Green Tewin Welwyn Hertfordshire AL6 0LX

www.tewinorchard.co.uk

Contents

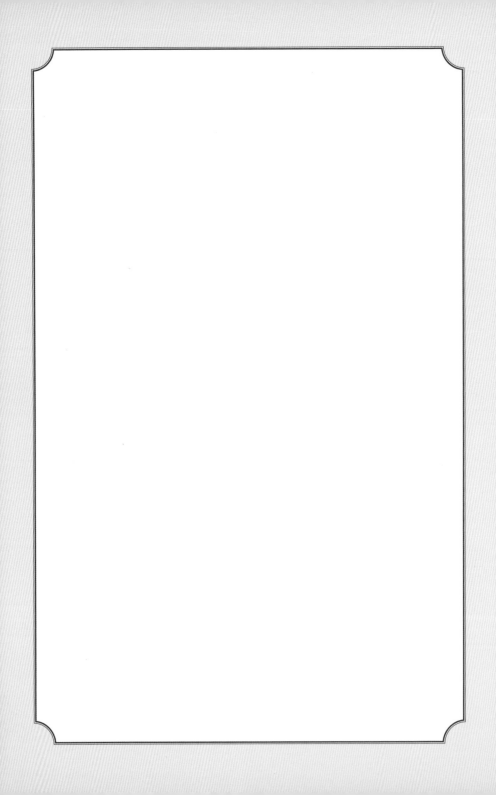

Chapter 1
Goodbye to the orchard

"I can hear something, Snore."

"Let me listen."

The young Badger moved quietly to the tunnel entrance. He sniffed out into the evening air.

"Man!"

"They must be coming back for us," said Snap. "Quick, to the back entrance."

The two Badgers ran along the dark tunnel and came to a narrow opening. The smell of Man was strong now.

"Follow me!" cried Snap.

They rushed out into the damp woodland and at once a cry went up from behind them. Three men had come to the sett. One threw a large pair of scissor-like tongs after the Badgers and another fired a gun, but both missed by yards in the darkness.

"Never known Badgers run from their sett," said one man.

"May have been from another one," said the man who fired the gun. "I told you it was a daft time to come up here."

"Daft to leave it any later. Next weekend the others would have dug them out and made all the money. You and your gun. They're worth more alive than as pelts."

"Well, that's the lot, unless we can find those two again. As we're here, we might as well dig just to be sure there are none left below ground."

The Badgers separated down well-used, secret paths in the dense bracken. Although the wood had been reduced to a narrow strip, the undergrowth provided ample cover.

It was not far to the southern edge of the trees. Snore stopped and listened intently, nose raised to test the air. The whiskers on his black and white face twitched and his moist, grey nostrils opened and closed tensely.

I'm well clear of them now, he thought. Wonder where Snap is.

He stared up into his beloved tree tops and his body gradually relaxed. There was only a slight breeze, but he continued to sniff the air for traces of Man.

They may come up the main track, he pondered. Anyway, I'll hear them. Nothing to do but wait now.

He closed his eyes and breathed in the scents of the wood. The air was heavy with the pollen of high summer and the familiar aroma of leaf mould drifted up from his fresh footprints along the path. A sudden feeling of happiness surged through his body. He had always loved to emerge from the dark tunnels into the evening air. It would give him a sense of joy to leave the closed world underground, with its tensions and squabbles, to enter the exciting haunts above. He laughed to himself as a Robin landed beside him at a footprint and then flew off, startled to see the young Badger.

Snore scratched at his neck and looked up at the complex pattern of branches and foliage which seemed to reach over and shelter him. He longed to climb the trees and often dreamed of living in one of the old oaks, safe from Men, never leaving the wood.

On the lower, eastern border, Snap ambled along the bank of a black, fouled stream, muttering to himself. His mind was filled with a mixture of hatred and fear for the Men. He snarled and hit out at a wide bracken frond which hung across the path. It danced back and forth as if mocking him.

There were sounds of voices from the road ahead and Snap pushed out of sight into a thicket of elder and brambles.

"Never any peace and quiet," he growled.

Snore stood directly below a high Beech tree and gazed at the curious spiral of boughs that thrust out from the central trunk.

I wonder...

"Hello Snore."

Snore spun round. It was the old Hare.

"Men are in the wood, Harry!" hissed Snore. "You must look out, they came after Snap and me."

The Hare laughed.

"I'm tired of looking out. Warmish, isn't it?"

Harry had a long, cheerful face which nodded slightly as he spoke. His greying ears swivelled constantly to cover every possible direction for sound. The habit was subconscious and had developed from a lifetime of caution.

"I love the wood when it's warm," said Snore. "Isn't it a wonderful place, despite everything?"

Harry smiled.

"Used to be a great deal better," he said with a sniff. "It is all Syringes and Boxes round here these days and they are not content to stay round the rubbish tips where they belong. Come and see what Man is up to now."

The foliage gave a dark, irregular frame to the view beyond the wood. Lights flashed on in the distance and the red of the setting sun caught the higher leaves and edged them with a fiery glow.

"The orchard's going next," said Harry.

Snore started.

"I didn't know that. What's happening?"

"I told Snap," the Hare went on. "They're taking down the old trees and planting young ones in concrete sheds. What with the roads, houses and new animals we are surrounded now."

Below them, the orchard trees led away towards a long, low, white house. Next to this, the first of the sheds was under construction and several felled trees lay across the open track which led to the house. A bonfire smouldered lazily nearby. They caught the scent of burning apple branches.

"My last field, Snore. Mind you, I don't care any more." He waved over his shoulder. "They will get me soon. I'm old and tired nowadays."

"Cheer up!" cried Snore. "You're as bad as Snap. He never looks on the bright side of things!"

"Can't blame him."

"But we must try to. Things may get better."

Harry smiled again, unaware of the constant, gentle nod of his old head. He looked at Snore's friendly eyes and the bright, eager expression on his face.

"So young. Your first summer."

The buzzing sound of a Syringe made Snore jump. Harry sighed and grumbled under his breath.

"It's coming over here."

The Syringe hovered noisily around them. It had a very thin nose with yellow and black striped body. The colours vibrated with the rapid beating of the wings and made Snore blink. At last it darted out of the trees and flew across the orchard.

"They'll be living with us in the wood next," said Snore.

"Only a matter of time. I was chased by a dog one morning and a Box the same afternoon. It just isn't natural. I once visited one of the tips and do you know, it must have been about a mile wide. Boxes everywhere! I was soon off!"

Leaves moved by a fallen oak and Snap appeared.

"Hello, Harry." Snap ignored his brother.

"Looking at your orchard?"

"My orchard! Hah! Yes, building's started."

Snap sighed deeply.

"I expect that he's told you, men are after us again. Even took a shot tonight."

Harry nodded and again grumbled under his breath.

"I hope they don't dig out the tunnels," said Snore, quietly.

"Of course they will," grunted Snap.

Harry shook his head.

"I should leave the wood while you can. Both of you. I'm staying. Too old. But you youngsters ought to go. There's nobody else now."

Snore stared up into the trees as an awful feeling of sadness gripped him.

If only the sett has been left alone...

Chapter 2
On the run

"Look at that!" growled Snap.

The sett had been dug out along every bend and twist of the tunnels. It was only a small sett, and the random structure of paths, junctions and three big chambers seemed even smaller when seen opened and from above.

"Destroyed," said Snore. "Why?"

"Harry was right. We should go tonight. There's nothing left here."

They turned away from their ruined birthplace. It had survived for less than a year, but served as a brief sanctuary when the main sett was destroyed. Snore ran just behind Snap and kept glancing at the wood on either side of the path. Every tree and shrub was familiar to him.

Will I ever see these again?

They came to a hedge bordering a busy road. Snap turned to his brother.

"Now don't blubber, but I must tell you something. We are probably the last Badgers in Britain."

"What do you mean, blubber!" cried Snore, although he felt very unhappy inside. "How do you know we are the last, anyway?"

"Old Boar Bill told me, the last time I saw him."

Snore stared at the ground.

"Did he tell you anything else?" he said.

"Just one thing. He could remember being told by his great grandfather, many years ago, that a wood was left near London. When he came west with the last southern Badgers, he heard that some of our kind still survived there, although the new animals may have taken over by now."

"Then we must find this wood," said Snore brightly.

"Silly Snore!" laughed Snap scornfully. "Easy to say 'find it', but how do you propose to do that? Everything's concrete now. It would be hard enough to find London!"

Snore said nothing. He pushed through the hedge and on to the concrete pavement beyond. Snap followed slowly.

It was now dark and street lights were bright above. Lights were also set into the side of the kerb to flood the road surface and this gave the impression of a misty yellow river winding away into the distance.

We must find the wood, Snore repeated to himself.

There were no humans to be seen as the young Badgers made their way along the pavement, but cars and lorries rushed past. A large, dark shape gradually appeared ahead. It was a lorry parked near a cafe.

"I once heard that lorries go to London on this road," said Snore as he paused by the huge lorry tyre.

"Well?" said Snap. "We don't know where this one is

going..."

He was cut short by a sound. Two men had emerged from the cafe and were coming slowly towards them, talking.

In a few seconds, Snore was on the back of the lorry. He pushed his way under a black plastic cover. Then his face reappeared and he hissed down to Snap, "Come on!"

Snap hesitated, then reluctantly clambered up and over the back.

"I should never have followed you along the road!" he muttered as he joined Snore.

There were sounds from the front and the lorry engine came to life. Snap started to complain loudly again. They covered their ears, then closed their eyes as the lorry pulled out into the traffic stream.

Across the sides was written:

WEST COUNTRY - LONDON ORCHARDS LIMITED

Chapter 3
A delivery of apples

The two Badgers sat on crates of apples under the cover. They ate the pale green fruit from one of the crates and dozed off as the long journey continued into the night.

From time to time Snore gazed down at the curious yellow road rushing away behind them. All he could see seemed yellow. Cars with yellow headlights would speed past, sometimes flashing smaller yellow lights as they overtook the lorry. He turned to Snap.

"How do they grow apples on concrete?"

No reply.

"Well?"

"They grow them in huge concrete sheds, safe from insects and Badger cubs!"

Snap was still angry and would say no more.

Snore awoke with a start at dawn.

We must be near London.

Tall, dark buildings surrounded them. Roads lit with pink lights joined their yellow route, but the lorry drove steadily on. People appeared here and there and Snore began to tremble slightly.

Snap looked out.

"See, Snap. It's morning and we are in London!"

"If this is London, we were very lucky."

Finally the lorry drove into a huge market area, filled

with noise. The lights here were brighter than the
yellow ones on the road. Vans and lorries, all made of
the same brilliant metal, drove into and out of tall steel
buildings from a wide, three-lane road.

"Jump down as soon as we stop," said Snap.

They came to a halt in a large loading bay. The
Badgers dropped quickly on to the concrete and hurried
across to some plastic boxes. They crouched down in
the shadows, well hidden from view. The smells of fruit
and Man filled their nostrils again as Hoversorters
distributed boxes to other bays.

It was an hour before the lorry left and a small van
arrived. Snore listened carefully to what two workmen
said.

"Tom wants a few apples. He's going up North today
with tomatoes and potatoes."

"Right, you can have a couple of these crates."

The van was open at the back and loaded high with
boxes. One of the men added two metal crates and then

climbed inside the cabin. He started the engine, but
continued to talk to the other man through the window.

"We must try this one!" said Snore.

"Why?" replied Snap. "How do we know if it will go
near the wood?"

"We'll have to take pot luck!"

Snore crawled from under the boxes and paused. The
men were still talking. Snap joined him. When all
seemed safe, they hurried across and boarded the van.

"There's nowhere to hide!" exclaimed Snap.

"Just keep down!"

They squeezed between the two large crates in the
centre of the load and kept their heads out of view of
the wide cabin window.

A few moments later the van drove off. The man who
had been talking to the driver waved and then looked
startled.

"Hey! You've got something on the crates!"

But his voice was drowned in the noise from the
loading bays and the van was soon out of the market
area, heading north along a blue tarmac road.

When the van was clear of London, Snore and Snap
kept a careful look-out for any signs of the wood. They
were now on a fast open motorway, but for as far as the
eye could see there were buildings and factories. The
sun was rising above a grey, monotonous landscape.

A wide sign with symbols for food and services
appeared on the side of the road. The van began to slow

down and a light on its left side flashed repeatedly.

"It must be stopping!" said Snore.

Snap groaned.

"This means trouble."

"I wish you wouldn't fuss so much," growled Snore.

"We may be miles away from the wood and now we're going towards houses."

The van turned into a side road. It led up a slight hill to a wide group of buildings, surrounded by parked cars and lorries.

"Heads down!" said Snore.

"I knew we should have waited..."

The noise of the engine ceased as the van came to a halt. The driver stepped out, yawning, slowly stretched each arm and reached inside the cabin for his jacket. He felt in a pocket and took out a plastic wallet. The sounds of each action were listened to with nervous attention by the Badgers.

What is he doing?

I warned him, but would he listen...?

Snore and Snap lay flat against the boxes, unable to see the driver.

The door banged.

Silence.

Gone?

Footsteps.

Here we go.

The driver walked slowly round the side of the van.

As he reached the back he glanced at the load. It was a habit, to see that nothing had moved.

For a moment he didn't notice the two animals. They lay so still. Then he stopped and stared.

"What are..."

"Come on!"

Snore jumped over the side. Snap followed.

"Oi! Stop!"

They kept under the line of parked vehicles. The strong smell from the oil and fuel stains made Snap cough and sneeze.

"Come on! Come on!" yelled Snore.

The man was on his hands and knees to see where they had gone. People approached.

"Can you help to catch some animals? They're going towards that end, underneath."

Snore saw feet appear ahead. A face, upside down, then another. He turned and scrambled into the daylight. Snap arrived beside him.

Men and women were advancing from both sides, laughing and shouting with hands reaching out towards them.

Snore ran towards an old wire fence across the car park. Behind it stood blocks of houses.

"We'll be caught over there!" shouted Snap.

Snore found a gap in the wire. A lorry had reversed into it at one time and broken the mesh. He pushed through, kicking away a tangle of wire round his feet.

"Quickly! Mind that wire."

Snap was not so nimble.

"I'm stuck!"

The wire tightened on Snap's foot as he struggled to get free.

Sounds of laughing, shouting and squealing came closer.

Snore thrust at Snap and they fell back on to the concrete. Snore then clawed at the wire, pulled it away from the swollen skin and forced Snap back into the gap. Suddenly hands clutched at Snore's back and pulled at his hair.

Noise filled Snore's ears to a level he could no longer stand. In a fury, he turned and snarled. The sounds subsided. He bit the nearest hand with a quick decisive snap.

The sounds changed. An exaggerated, silly scream. Exclamations and shocked words. Snore jumped through the gap in the fence and was gone.

Chapter 4
Scrumping

Between each block of houses were small overgrown gardens. Rubbish had been dumped in scattered heaps all round the abandoned flower and vegetable beds.

Snore and Snap ran across a narrow path to the nearest hedge where they found a way through long grass and hurried into the first garden.

"Keep going!"

The next garden was full of brambles and plastic car tyres. An old concrete shed had fallen across the wire fence and broken two of the posts. They scurried over debris and large docks, through three more gardens. All were overgrown.

The voices of people in the motorway park died away. Snore and Snap crawled into an old shed and sat on some sacks.

They slowly calmed down.

"How's your foot?" asked Snore.

"All right."

As their breathing eased, they listened carefully. There was an unreal stillness in the air.

"It's funny. There's no smell of people round these houses."

Snore opened the door slightly and looked out.

"Everything looks disused, like a Badger sett that has

not been lived in for ages."

"You wait!" grumbled Snap. "They'll try to find us. The stench of humans...!" He rubbed his foot. "I know what you mean, though. I don't think people live here any more."

"What shall we do about the van?"

"Blow the van! I'm hungry."

Snore nosed out of the shed.

"We should find something to eat in these old gardens. Can you walk easily on your foot?"

Snap nodded.

They paused at the door. Snore sniffed the air for human scent. A gentle wind stirred the undergrowth. There was no other movement.

"All clear."

A vast bed of brambles and stinging nettles hid the next fence. They made their way cautiously through to a row of old poles. The ground had been cultivated for runner beans, but a few strands of nylon cord trailing from the poles were all that survived.

"I'll dig around," said Snore.

Snap found some blackberries.

"Nothing!" muttered Snore a few minutes later. "Not even an old potato!"

"Have some of these."

They sat and ate the berries.

"Looks like an apple tree close to the building block." Snore pointed.

"I shouldn't go up there. Somebody might see you."

Snore looked round at the houses. The windows were all broken and the rooms appeared dark and lifeless. The only sounds came from rusty hinges as doors and window frames squeaked gently to and fro in the breeze.

"I cannot see anyone. Won't be a moment."

He crept slowly to the tree and picked up four of the apples lying in the long grass. A Wasp buzzed lazily away close-by. Snore turned to Snap and pointed at the Wasp.

"Look, that's not a Syringe!"

Snap nodded impatiently, certain that at any moment

a vast horde of men would rush out from the houses and catch them.

Snore picked a fifth apple with the result that he dropped the others.

"You'll get caught!"

When he had all five apples balanced precariously in his arms, Snore walked nonchalantly back to Snap.

"Thanks. You do take some risks, though."

"We seem to live off apples!"

"Hm. Not bad."

Snore laughed.

"At least these were not grown in concrete sheds!"

"Not far off," smiled Snap. "These are a better colour, but you can hardly call these tiny gardens orchards. The houses must hide most of the light."

A bird flew over them. It paused in the apple tree and gave a brief song.

"Blackbird!" said Snore. "There it goes. That's something in all this brickwork and concrete."

"Yes. And I think I saw a Butterfly earlier. Before that Wasp. These old gardens must support a few still."

They finished the apples. Snore stood up and stared hard at the buildings.

"If all these gardens are deserted, we could hide here for as long as we wanted to."

"But we wouldn't find the wood, or the Badgers," said Snap.

"No. Quite true. I can't wait to see them."

Snore thought for a moment.

"Let's explore this house. It might make a good hiding place this evening."

"Possibly," said Snap with a frown, "but be careful. There may be people still about, or even traps inside."

Snore led past the apple tree and up some steps to a doorway. The door hung from one hinge. It left a triangular gap clear for the Badgers to squeeze through.

Heaps of bricks and rubble covered the dusty floor. An old sink unit and empty cupboard were the only features of the first room. The air was damp and the cracked walls glistened with moisture.

"Look, Snap. A way upwards."

"Careful!"

The staircase was broken in places by falls of plaster. Peeling paper hung in weird curls all round and the walls were stained with the faded colours of age and neglect.

"Can you see anything?"

Snore was at a window.

"Only the other buildings and strips of gardens. We shall see much more higher up."

They climbed past two more floors to the top of the house and looked over the roof tops.

"Houses, houses, houses! Nothing but old houses," said Snore. "I wonder if they are all empty."

"I expect we can see the motorway from here."

Snap went to another window.

"No. Perhaps from the next room."

Snore joined him.

"Yes. Look down there."

"Those must be the cars and lorries in the park. I think the van has gone."

"Hard to tell."

"The road curves away, across there."

People moved to and from the vehicles. They were

the only sign of life away from the busy motorway.

"Look!" Snore exclaimed suddenly. "Trees!"

"Where?"

"There, there!"

In the distance, amongst a complex landscape of

towers, factories and houses was a line of dark trees.

"The wood! It must be!"

Snore jumped up and down at the window with excitement. Snap beamed at his brother.

"Calm down! We're not there yet !"

"Well, what shall we do now?" asked Snore.

"Go there as soon as possible."

"We must get another van, then. Down in the park."

"No." said Snap. "It would be safer to walk."

"But we'd be seen. Or get lost. It's still a long way on foot."

"Not if we go at night and keep close to the motorway. It goes right towards the trees, see?"

"At night! A van would be so much quicker," insisted Snore. "Better fun, too."

They looked at each other and then out of the window again. Both sighed deeply.

"Another thing. How can we stop a van by the wood?"

Snore thought for a moment.

"I don't know. We'd think of something."

"Come on, let's see how far we can walk in daylight."

Chapter 5
A delivery of Badgers

"Keep under cover," whispered Snore.

They were opposite the wire fence next to the motorway park.

Snore edged along the side of the end garden and into some bushes. Snap looked round carefully as he followed.

"If we stay next to the motorway fence we are bound to find the wood," said Snore.

"Eventually," commented Snap.

Beyond the bushes was another row of houses. They walked silently into a narrow courtyard.

"What's that smell?" said Snore.

"Dead water, I think."

They pushed through long grass and mint to a fence smothered in honeysuckle. Its soft scent was overpowered by a stronger odour.

"Phew! There must be an old pond ahead."

Below the honeysuckle the ground fell away into an open, grassy bank.

"Oh no!"

Snore sat down.

"What is it?"

They were above a motionless, black canal. The water was choked with rubbish of every kind and the

walls were stained dark green.

"We can't get across that," said Snore, with a faintly triumphant air.

The canal led away to the far left for as far as the eye could see. Old footbridges, built to link the houses at regular intervals, had fallen down and now hung twisted and useless in the stagnant water. To the right, the canal went under the motorway, but a high fence above a vertical wall prevented any passage across.

"We will have to go back to the gap in the motorway fence and cross the water on the bank up there," said Snap.

"Yes," said Snore.

The park was busy. It was approaching lunch-time, but nobody noticed the Badgers as they looked through the fence.

"It's dangerous here," said Snap. "I wish there was another hole further along."

Snore tensed.

"The van!" he whispered with excitement. "It's still there. Look!"

Snap sniffed.

"Where? It all looks different to me."

"By that big lorry. The lorry wasn't there before, but the van is in the same place."

"Yes, I see. So what?"

"We can get on the open back again!"

"What! Are you mad! The driver would see us at once."

"Not if we hide by the lorry until he sits in the front part!"

Snap shook his head slowly.

"Very clever, I must say. But, as I have said before, how can we stop the van at the wood ?"

"Bang on the roof, or something. If, when we reach the wood, we show our faces at his window, he's bound to stop to try to catch us again."

"No doubt he will succeed, too."

"We are just as likely to be caught on the side of the motorway, crossing the canal, day or night. They make lights at night, too, remember."

Snap shrugged his shoulders and sat down with his back to the fence. At that moment, the van driver appeared. He walked along the line of vehicles, his hair newly cut and with a carrier bag full of shopping. He stopped by the back of the van and checked the boxes carefully. Then he turned towards the fence.

Snore drew back out of sight.

The man went round to the cabin and climbed inside.

"See!" hissed Snore, "we've missed our chance!"

Snap reluctantly turned to look through the gap. The driver began to reverse the van so that he could turn past the lorry. It backed further and further towards the fence.

"We still have a chance! Please come!" pleaded

Snore.

Snap would not move. Snore ran out from the fence across the hot tarmac towards the back of the van. He scrambled on board and turned round, waving.

Snap hesitated at the fence. His brother beckoned frantically. He began to run, but the van was clear of the lorry and drove forward and away. As it accelerated, Snap reached Snore's out-stretched paws. He swung up side ways and they tumbled over amongst the boxes.

The van joined the motorway traffic stream as Snore and Snap sat up.

"We must be ready to stop the van," said Snore. "The wood isn't all that far away."

"I'm not looking forward to this," said Snap. He looked about him. Buildings, cars, lorries. All rushing past in the sunlight. Then at last a wide area of trees appeared. The low, uneven tree tops stood out clearly from the tall blocks of houses and concrete towers.

"Nearly there!" said Snore.

Snap stood up as they drew level with the trees.

"I'll do the banging. You stand by the edge there."

"Good for you, Snap!"

Snap climbed over the boxes. Standing on tip-toe, he started to bang on the roof. The horrified face of the driver appeared at the window and the van slowed down.

"Get ready to jump!" shouted Snap.

Snore crouched on the edge of the van and looked
down at the grassy bank which ran down from the
motorway towards the wood. Snap gave a final bang on
the roof and came to join Snore. As he reached the side,
the man looked back and the van suddenly began to
gain speed.

"I'll bang again," said Snap. He climbed back to the
cabin roof.

"Do be careful, Snap!"

"Don't worry!"

He banged for all he was worth and the driver turned
towards the side of the road once more. He scowled
back at them as he pulled up.

"Jump!" shouted Snap.

Snore held his breath and leapt on to the grass. He

rolled over and over down the bank, then scrambled to his feet and looked back. There was no van. No Snap. Then he caught a brief glimpse of them going faster and faster away.

By the time Snore had reached the top of the bank, the van was a tiny shape in the distance. He could see his brother at the cabin roof again, but all blurred with the busy motorway traffic as they rushed northwards.

Chapter 6
The Marble Eater

A rough track, next to the grass bank of the motorway, led towards the first of the trees. Snore sat down and wiped his eyes.

The wood stood dark and strange before him. He looked back at the motorway. No Snap. Just cars and lorries streaming noisily past.

"I must find the Badgers," said Snore out loud. He walked towards the trees.

I hope I don't get lost.

He hesitated.

What tall trees. So dark, but not friendly-dark like my trees at home; black, mysterious. Those must be Pinelons, or whatever the name is.

The Pinelons were joined in lines to each other by long strands which dipped and hung from each tree before rising to the top of the next.

How can I find the Badgers in such a big wood? Perhaps there are lots of them and they will find me.

"I am over here!" shouted Snore.

Silence. Not even an echo. Just the steady drone of the motorway. He walked past smaller trees which were rounded and joined in a curious way. The branches formed a complex network of shapes and shut out the sun from the path below.

These trees are not like the ones round the old sett at home. I wonder why there are no leaves. I wish Snap was here. He doesn't look on the bright side of things, but he is very brave. I bet he would know what to do...

Tap, tap, tap.

Snore stopped and peered through the trees.

Tap, tap, tap. The sound was coming nearer. Snore paused behind a low branch and looked to see what was making the noise.

It must be a Marble. Bright red with touches of blue.

It came bouncing through the trees towards Snore and then turned off along a path away to his left. Tap, tap, tap.

Harry told me about these.

The Marbles had spread out from the rubbish dumps and towns more slowly than the Syringes, but were not far behind. The animal had a round body no bigger than Snore's pad and bounced on two tiny legs. Even in the half light of the wood, its colour seemed to glow. Then another Marble came past, tap, tap, tap, after the first.

I might as well follow them, but what are they doing here in the wood? They belong round the towns. Perhaps they know where the Badgers are.

Snore quietly trailed the Marbles through the trees. More appeared ahead and then he found himself overlooking a small clearing with a large Marble Hill in the centre. Scores of Marbles bounced into and out of entrances in the side of the heap. Snore watched, fascinated by the colour and noise. They seemed to be endlessly busy, but all of a sudden they fell silent and the movement ceased.

I must have frightened them. No, wait. What's that sound?

Through the trees, just beyond the heap, with a slow, steady waddle appeared a heavy, aggressive-looking animal. It had a long thin nose which wavered about the undergrowth as it walked. Snore drew closer to the tree trunk. The clearing was now deserted.

The strange animal sniffed loudly round the Marble Hill. Then a Marble appeared on the edge of the

clearing and began to bounce towards the heap. The heavy creature swung its long nose round just as the newcomer noticed that something was wrong.

"Squeak!"

There was a loud snort and the Marble rattled up the odd nose. Snore rushed from behind the tree and shouted:

"Go away, you brute!"

The animal was so surprised that it sneezed and the Marble it had just sniffed up shot out across the ground. The Marble jumped to its feet and rushed for home.

For a moment neither Snore nor the Marble Eater moved. Then the animal snorted again and began to waddle towards Snore.

"I don't like you," it hissed.

When Snore stopped running, he found himself on the edge of a wide path which curved out of sight in both directions.

I'll try this way.

All was silent. Not even the motorway sounds now. He made his way carefully, keeping close to the edge of the path.

If only there was something to eat! What kind of wood is this, with no food anywhere. Wish I'd kept an apple or two!

It was mid-afternoon and the wood was colder than before. The path kept turning first one way and then the other, so that Snore could not see where it led. He hurried along, looking for footprints and other signs of Badgers.

A distant sound made Snore pause and listen, ear to the ground. Vibrations ran along the path, as if a group of heavy animals was passing nearby. Gradually all movement ceased.

Perhaps they were Badgers. I should have shouted, but perhaps they were not... surely there are not just new animals here?

Snore trembled for a few moments, looking at the endless rows of trees all round the path. It was as if he was enclosed by walls of trees. Even hunger didn't tempt him to enter their ominous shadows. The path widened further on and bushes grew in patches on the border. Snore knelt by a bush and looked for berries and nuts below the rounded branches.

Not a thing! I'm so hungry.

He suddenly saw a dark shape appear by a bush, along the path.

A Badger? No, the shape seems wrong, too small and rounded. A Box ? Harry hated Boxes, but never said what they looked like.

Snore moved out of sight and then looked again, but the animal had gone. He felt very frightened now. Where are the old animals? Then a soft buzzing sound distracted him. It grew louder as something rushed past through the air.

Just a Syringe.

He tried to follow the animal with his eyes, but lost it against the trees. Then another and another came past, flying to a hole in the base of a tree.

Snore approached carefully. A soft, sweet smell came from inside. The hole was just large enough for Snore to feel inside with one pad. He gave a sharp pull and part of the tree fell away.

"Buzzz!" came the indignant sound from inside. A box-shaped nest was suspended across the hollow trunk. Angry Syringes, crowding round, buzzed with outraged fury. They flew at Snore as he pulled away the nest and ran down the path.

Syringes swarmed after him and dived to sting his body.

"Food! Sweet food at last... ow! Go away! oh! You horrid creatures!"

It was no good. More and more Syringes joined in the chase and Snore took a final delicious bite before throwing the remains of the nest into the trees. Still they would not leave him. It was as if he had become attached to a noisy motor which was out of control and would not stop. All fear of meeting other animals had gone. He took no notice of the winding path as he ran deeper into the wood.

Finally, the last one gave up. Snore stopped and looked round to make sure he was alone again. His ears still buzzed with the noise and he groaned as he sat down at the edge of the path. Something had caught on his leg and he pulled it away from the hair. It was a sticky piece of nest. He nibbled it sadly.

All that for one small meal!

His head ached as he glanced up. The sky was darkening rapidly now and the trees began to merge into strange shapes.

"Snap! Snap! Come and help me!"

Silence, not even an echo. It was all so lonely.

The weird white shape of a bird drifted from a Pinelon nearby. It stared downwards through round, forlorn eyes. Snore drew back into the trees and watched as it passed over. Its body was cylindrical, like the tree branches, but shorter and more rounded. The white wings beat slowly up and down as it flew over. It gave a deep "Hoo-ooo" and vanished into the trees again.

An hour later, with lazy wing beats, the bird came over the path once more, but Snore was asleep, out of sight under the black trees.

Chapter 7

A throw of the Dice

There was no dawn chorus. No joyful bird song at first light.

Snore slept on, occasionally trembling or twitching as he dreamed.

"Hello Badgers! I have found you at last," he would mutter, and roll over with sleepy happiness.

Two small animals finally woke him. They were chasing each other under the trees and ran over his back, playing hide-and-seek amongst his hair. Each had a square, white body with black spots on each side. They ran on little feet, waving long thin tails and suddenly one squeaked. Snore jumped up, rubbing his eyes. The animals fell to the ground and hurried away unnoticed.

Morning! Today I must find the Badgers. They may have walked right past me in the night. If only the wood was friendly at night, like the one at the old sett.

He wandered stiffly along the path and began to search for some food. He looked out for more Syringe nests in the trees, but shuddered at the thought of being chased again.

At first Snore was puzzled by small holes in some of the trees. None were as big as the Syringe nest holes and all lacked the sweet, appealing aroma of food inside.

Then he saw a thin, pointed creature at work. It was running in a circle on the side of a tree, drilling an opening with its long, twisted nose.

"Hello."

The animal stopped and frowned at Snore.

"Hello."

No movement or sound.

"Why are you animals so unfriendly?"

It began to drill into the tree once more.

A few paces further along the two animals that had played on his back ran on to the path, stopped and stared at Snore. He smiled down at them.

"You look comic!"

To his surprise they smiled back. He knelt down.

"You must be Dice. Where do you live? Harry, my old friend, thought you came from the towns and rubbish pits."

The Dice turned to each other and giggled.

"Well?" laughed Snore.

"We, we live..."

They dissolved into more squeaky giggles.

"I am looking for the Badgers." Snore spoke very slowly. "Do you know where they live?"

The Dice looked at each other again.

"Badgers?" one squeaked.

"Yes, like me."

"Never seen one. Not like you. Can you jump?"

"Jump? I think so. Why?"

"We can, look!"

The Dice jumped round Snore's legs, laughing louder and louder.

"Slow down!" cried Snore. "Have you never heard of the Badgers?"

The Dice stopped and huddled together, whispering loudly.

"Speak up!" said Snore.

"Squeak up! Squeak up!" shrieked one and set the other off into fits of laughter again.

"You're too silly for words!"

"For words! Backwards!" More chuckles.

They calmed down and grinned up at Snore, their eyes still full of excitement.

"Are Badgers big animals?"

"Yes. Like Foxes and Otters. Aren't there Hares, Rabbits and Squirrels round here?"

"We hide from the big animals. They might eat us. Will you eat us?"

"No! But I do want to find the Badgers."

"Let's ask the Screws."

The Dice scurried along the path.

"Come on!" one squeaked back.

A shadow passed over Snore and he looked up startled. The Dice did not notice. High in the sky was a bird with wide, rectangular wings. It circled round in the sun and began to follow Snore as he made his way along the path.

"Why follow me, silly bird?"

The Dice were chattering at one of the Screw holes in a tree. At last a long nose appeared and looked out.

"Screwy," said one, "do you know the Badgers?"

The Screw eyed Snore from the hole and sniffed.

There was a long silence and then it vanished back inside the tree.

"Come back!" squeaked the Dice.

There was a pause. Then the Screw reluctantly stared out through its cold eyes, frowned and mumbled to the Dice.

Snore could hear nothing, but patiently waited. The large bird still circled slowly round and made him feel uncomfortable. At last the Screw spoke out loud.

"I think Badgers used to live over there." It twitched its nose towards the distant bend of the path. "But," it wrinkled up the long nose in a very unfriendly way, "I'm not sure, they may not have done and you must not quote me on that."

"Thank you for helping..." began Snore, but the nose had gone.

The Dice looked up and Snore noticed that the bird was at a lower height than before. The sun flashed and shimmered round the black wings.

"And thank..." The Dice shouted "KITE!" and ran away into the dark trees without another squeak.

Snore hurried on. The path widened, but the wood looked as thick and dark as ever.

Round and round above. I shall have to run into the wood if it attacks.

Glancing back, Snore could see the Kite's eyes now. They glared down without blinking as the bird came lower in slow circles.

Snore began to run. Faster. A turning in the path appeared ahead. He ran down this and the trees opened into a clearing. The Kite dipped downwards and the

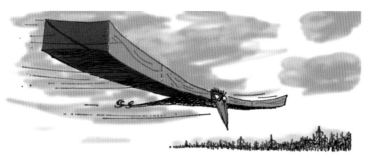

wind whistled through the blunt, taut wings as it fell into a steep dive.

I must get under the trees!

He ran towards a tall Pinelon on the edge of the clearing, but an old rut in the path caught his foot. He sprawled forwards as the Kite reached the tree-tops in its hideous, screaming dive.

The noise stopped and Snore looked up to see the Kite sweep upwards into the sky. It let out a furious scream and at that moment Snore noticed the man, standing by the Pinelon.

Oh no!

All thoughts of the Kite vanished. Snore ran into the clearing and then scrambled up a young tree growing apart from the dense woodland.

Go away!

The man slowly advanced and then spoke.

"Hello!"

Snore peered down.

Why so friendly? Is he trying to trick me? I'll drop sticks on him!

"Hello!"

It was difficult to see the man through the branches. Snore leaned back.

"H-hello."

As Snore spoke he somehow lost his balance and fell backwards. In a moment he was tumbling through the branches and landed with a thump!

"Are you all right?" asked the man anxiously.

"Hm! If you hurt me, all the Badgers will come and get you."

"I like Badgers and will not harm you. It's wonderful to see you. I thought the Badgers had been driven off by the new animals."

Snore did not know what to say. It was so confusing.

"Are you hungry?"

"Yes!"

"Share my breakfast, then. I always bring it with me on a fine morning. It tastes so much better outdoors."

The man untied a large box from a curious load of odds and ends on his back. They sat on a bank near the path and shared eggs, buttered rolls and cheese. Snore gave happy grunts and ate quickly.

"My name is Wallace, but everyone calls me 'Old Man'."

"I am Snore. Everyone calls me Snore."

"What are you doing here?"

"I came with my brother hoping to find the Badgers. Men dug out all of us at home and we escaped to London. We were nearly caught later, but we got to the wood on the back of a van. Then Snap could not get off when I did and I came into the wood on my own."

"Snap?"

"He is my brother."

"I expect he got to the wood as well."

"I do miss him."

Old Man closed his empty food box and tied it to a piece of string hanging from his back.

"Why is the wood so horrible? I thought these animals lived in the rubbish tips and towns."

Old Man smiled.

"You mean the new animals. At one time, people

lived near here and all kinds of old tin cans, bottles and rubbish were dumped in the wood. This was the last wood - the 'Mysterious Greatwood' - and should have been kept clean, but soon there was little to see of the trees from the outside. People did not like to go into the wood or live here and most of them left. It was basically the same everywhere else. Rubbish of every kind. If there was a space, someone dumped something there. Some dumps cover five square miles of what was once open country.

"Things began to change. Some of the animals adapted to the new surroundings. They evolved colours and shapes to fit the conditions. An animal which looks like a tin-can will survive where tin-cans are more common than grass and bushes."

"What are tin-cans?" asked Snore.

Old Man explained and then continued.

"At present these creatures are spreading everywhere. The old animals survive in places, where the old trees and grass still grow, round gardens and mountains. The new animals seem to do well where the new trees, rubbish and concrete are. They are said to attack the old animals."

Snore thought for a moment.

"How did these peculiar trees come here?" he asked. "What happened to the old ones?"

"There are two types of trees in the wood now."

The Old Man turned and pointed.

"See the big ones. They are called Pinelons. Men developed them from natural woods and metals. Sounds incredible, but that is science for you! The result is a curious tin which actually grows and they were planted out to carry lines of cable to take electricity across the land.

"It was an experiment to make the ugly rows of metal cables look like trees, because it was too expensive to put the lines underground. But few people cared in the end, as the country was criss-crossed more and more. They are just an experiment which has fallen into disuse. Most of them are mature and the cables send down roots, like strawberry runners."

"I quite like them now, in a funny way," said Snore. "The others look so dark and grow so close together."

"Ugly, rigid shapes," agreed Old Man. "Mind you, some are made of wood! The scientists created a tree, from mixtures of the old ones, which grew in that very geometric way. It saved space. As land became so valuable, a means of growing wood in great density was very welcome to owners of forests. This sort not only grow close to each other with circular, ready to cut trunks, but sends up straight branches of almost perfectly round dimensions. Ready made for all sorts of uses. I came here to study the new animals living amongst the dumps and trees. All the silver birches and hornbeams have gone. Even the oaks. I am writing a book about the creatures and visit the wood to make

notes and drawings. They seem to live as well here as in the rubbish."

There was so much for Snore to try to understand.

"Can we find the Badgers?"

"I hope so. We must try later on."

Snore jumped up and laughed.

"We are going to find the Badgers! We are going to find the Badgers!" He ran about, laughing with happiness.

Old Man beamed. It was rare to see such an outburst of joy.

"Our best plan is to look round the old Badger sett."

"Where is that?"

"On the other side of this clearing."

The oddments on Old Man's back rattled and bumped as they walked. Snore felt relaxed for the first time since he had entered the wood.

"It seems a huge clearing, Old Man."

"Yes. There are several small sand pits at the far end. The Badgers made their sett into one of these. Nowadays the Boxes use it."

"Harry told me about Boxes," muttered Snore.

"They are big and reddish-brown. I have found that the best time to see them is in the afternoon or evening."

"Did you say that people had left their homes round the wood?"

"Yes. There were many troubles. The first great disaster was from the water supply. We call it 'pollution'. Man, you see, Snore, has covered the ground with either concrete or rubbish and made the air and water dirty."

"Dirty?"

"There's no better word for it. When the rivers, lakes and seas were filled with waste from factories and homes, all kinds of chemical changes took place. It took a long time, but when it eventually happened," Old Man threw up his hands, "disaster. Although that was nothing compared with The Virus."

"The Virus?"

"An illness people died from. There were several, we think and that was just the name that stuck. Like 'The

Plague' or 'Black Death'. Before your time and it's a
long story."

"Will the people come back to the wood?"

"I don't think so. They find these new trees
frightening. So dark. The houses are empty, so I doubt
if the wood will be visited much again. The motorway
is on the eastern border of the trees, as you know, but
nobody can park along there. It all came too late for the
countryside."

"Why don't they pull down the houses and bring back
the old sort of woods and fields?"

Old Man gave a deep sigh.

"I think they have forgotten how beautiful the
countryside used to be, Snore. Mind you, people do like
to see the birds in their little gardens. But that's about
all. The animals have gone and very few people are
interested in these new creatures."

"Gone? But what about the Badgers?"

"Perhaps they are still near here, but to be honest, I
have never found tracks. Not that I've explored very
thoroughly, mind." His eyes brightened. "I bet your
brother has found them!"

Snore fell silent.

I wish I knew. Good old Snap.

The Badger earths had sandy heaps of soil outside each
entrance.

"A couple look used, Snore."

Snore sniffed deeply into each tunnel, but there was

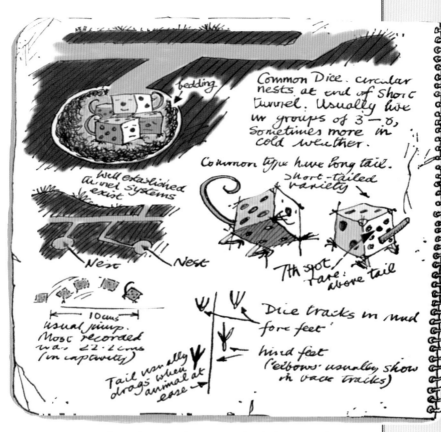

no friendly trace of Badgers. They searched the wood around the pits. Snore crawled under the trees and Old Man knelt to examine the narrow paths round the Pinelons.

At midday they sat down together above the sett.

"I am sorry, Snore. We can look again this afternoon."

"Snap was sure the Badgers came to this wood. He had been told that we might be the last if there were none here."

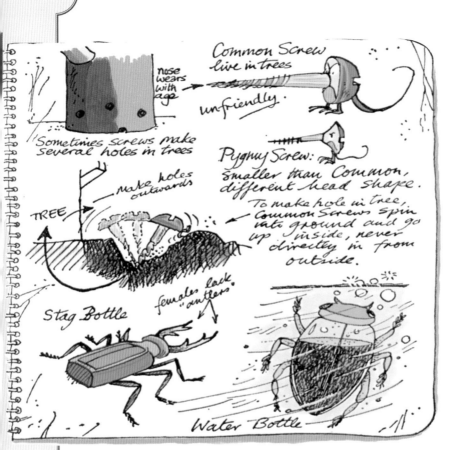

"Cheer up. We'll find them." Old Man changed the subject. "How many new animals have you seen in the wood?"

"Yesterday I shouted at a big animal eating the Marbles. He was awful."

"That would have been one of the Marble Eaters. What else?"

"Some big animals came near, but I only saw one for a moment before it was gone. Then I was attacked by

Syringes that stung like anything because I stole their nest! We had those round the wood at home.

"A big white bird flew over last night and this morning I asked some funny little spotted fellows if they'd seen the Badgers. They were the only friendly animals I met. They asked an unpleasant creature with a very long, thin nose and he pointed down the path. The great black bird chased me and I saw you!"

"You were lucky I frightened it, Snore. Let me show you my rough drawings. You may recognise a few 'friends'!"

Old Man untied the sketchbook from his back. Snore laughed at the drawings of the Dice and Screws, but frowned at the Scowl and Kite.

"Have there been many Robots along the paths?"

"Robots?" asked Snore.

"They replaced Rabbits."

Old Man turned the page and pointed.

"No. None of those." said Snore. "Wait, yes. The first animal I saw after the Marble Eater must have been one of those. I thought it was a Badger, but it was small and had a round back like this."

"They live in all parts of the wood. Very common. Mind you, the Boxes feed on them and they are very shy in daylight."

Old Man closed the book.

"Time for lunch. Would you like a cheese roll or two?"

Chapter 8
Plastic flowers

Snore finished the third cheese roll and scratched his elbow.

"Where do you live, Old Man?"

"I have a cottage on the border of the wood. When the weather is bad I work at home. I keep Dice and other animals to study in one of the rooms. They live in large containers with glass covers so that I can watch them easily."

"Are you afraid of the big animals in the wood?"

"No. The only large creatures here are the Boxes and some herds of Steer. They would never attack a man, unless, perhaps, they were cornered. They are the only two types of animals you need fear, now that the people have gone."

"And the big black bird!"

"Oh yes, the Kite. But they are easy to hide from in the trees. If they land on the ground, they need lots of space to fly off again."

"Do you think the Badgers are afraid of the Boxes and Steers?"

"Steer," corrected Old Man. "There must be a reason why the Badgers are hard to find now, Snore. It may have been because the wood changed. The new animals like these dark trees, but the old animals probably couldn't find enough food."

Snore looked at the sketchbook again.

"Are those the Steer?"

"Yes. There are also other animals you have not met."
He flicked over a few pages. "Those are Mats, those
Hats and this is the Tin Opener Bird which cuts holes in
the Pinelons and makes its nest in the trunk. When it

climbs inside it turns round and closes the door. The
male Green Hammer, that's him, has a big beak and
knocks on the Tin Opener's door. This annoys the Tin
Opener and it finally leaves the eggs and chases the
Green Hammer away. They are noisy, unfriendly birds.

"While they are flying round, the female Green
Hammer hops inside and lays one big egg with the
other eggs already in the nest. The Tin Opener returns
and in one week or so the Green Hammer chick hatches
and pushes out all the smaller eggs."

"Horrid!"

Old Man laughed.

"I discover new things about the animals almost every

day. Similar things have happened all over the World. In Africa, for example, the humans have great trouble from certain new animals found in the concrete jungles. One small animal consumes stored cement. They are called Cemites and have evolved from the old wood-eating Termites. The Concrites are the most damaging. Hundreds of them, in columns, will enter a building and eat their way through the concrete and bricks until whole floors and walls collapse as a fine powder of dust.

"I remember when a colony was brought to the splendid research centre at the London Zoo. They had to be guarded night and day, kept in a thick wooden chamber and fed on parts of walls from demolished houses. Still, enough of Concrites, we must now find these Badgers."

They walked round the pit and followed the path into the wood.

"Do you study the flowers, too?" asked Snore. "We had some at home."

"There is only one flower now in the wood itself," said Old Man. "Plastigro Daffodils spread from the rubbish heaps. Again, it was a case of men wanting a false ideal: the flower that grows and stays in bloom all the year round. They are always yellow."

"That does seem dull."

"Yes. Not a patch on real flowers. The trees are the same. No leaves. No colour, unless you count grey and black as colours. If only the Mysterious Greatwood had not been spoilt. The concrete around the wood could be dug up and planted with trees and grass. There are fewer and fewer people and more and more empty buildings." He sighed. "It has all come too late."

They searched one path after another, but there were no traces of Badgers. The paths all seemed the same. Snore felt desperate again.

Badgers! We are here! Snap! Snap!

No response.

"Let's go back to the clearing, Snore." Old Man had a patient, kindly voice. "It's mid-afternoon now and you can rest by the earths. We may see a Box later on."

Snore nodded. He was tired.

"Don't be sad, Snore, Snap will turn up. So will the Badgers."

He is just trying to cheer me up. But I know they're here. I can feel it. Old Man won't understand, but I can feel it.

Chapter 9
Box watching

"You should find Box watching exciting, Snore," said Old Man. "The wood has some colour at night, although the animals are still very shy if I am around. It is best if we are not too near the entrances to start with. At dusk we can move closer."

He sat down with a rattle of tins and boxes.

"Why do you carry all those things on your back?" asked Snore.

"Blowed if I know! Make an awful row, don't they." He reached round. "You know my food box." He picked up a net. "I catch little flying animals and water animals with this. These boxes are my Dice and Screw traps. I catch animals alive, you see, and release them afterwards."

"Why do you want to catch them?" asked Snore. He pushed open the small swing door at the front of one of the traps.

"It is for my study of the wood. I put a tiny ring on the leg of each animal. Every ring has a different number. I write down the type of animal, where I caught it and the number of the ring. In this tin I keep a spring balance for weighing them. When all is complete, I release the animal."

"I see," said Snore.

Poor Old Man. He must be mad.

"I may catch ten or twelve Dice in one night. Then I move the traps to another part of the wood. Sometimes I catch Dice and Screws with rings already on. I look at

the number, check in my note book and can then tell how far the animals travel."

"But what for?"

"For my book about the wood. You see, one day I hope to know all about the animals. In the old days, some people went to the woods to learn all about the old animals and plants. They told the other people that trees and animals should be given room to live. But there were too many humans. Even nature reserves and wildlife parks were built over.

"There just wasn't the space. The same thing may happen, for other reasons, in this new wood, but at least I want to try. This is all we have left of a woodland habitat, even though the new animals live elsewhere. You can't tell other people what should be done until you know yourself."

Snore was more interested. The trap fascinated him and he held it up to the light.

"How do you stop them from escaping through the door?"

"They find the chopped up garbage and refuse I leave as bait and hop inside. They step on to a piece of wire, just here, which releases the door. It swings down and closes the opening. A bar, see, this thing, holds it tight. They turn round and discover that there is no way out. This makes them angry at first, but they finally settle down in the grass and make a nest. Next morning I turn up."

"Did you say you kept some at home?"

"Yes, in the cottage. My animal room."

"How many have you got?"

"Too many! The Dice, you remember I told you, live in a series of small rooms with glass fronts. I keep adding bits. Even the tunnels which connect the containers together have glass tops so that I can see the Dice at all times. It is much easier to watch the small animals indoors."

"Do you feed your Dice ?"

"Oh yes. They eat everything, including the old sort of foods, like peanuts, oats, apples, water. They have food trays, but also make stores in their nests. The young Dice have only a few spots to start with. They increase in number as the Dice grow and usually stop at twenty-one. Some rare ones have white spots on black."

"White on black? That must look funny."

"If the Dice were always black," said Old Man with a grin, "you would think the white ones strange! There is endless variety in nature, Snore. Even now I have often wondered if Badgers have white on black faces or black on white! Do you know?"

Snore put his hand to his face and looked puzzled for a moment. Then:

"It feels like black on white!"

They both laughed, but suddenly Snore looked very sad.

"Cheer up."

"I wish I had little rooms and tunnels and Dice to watch."

"Snore! Most people think I'm mad to have such things. Mind you, I think they all like the aquarium."

"What's an aquarium?"

"A sort of indoor pond. I net water animals from the river just north of here, although at last the old fish are coming back there I'm glad to say. The aquarium is made of glass and filled with water. In this way all the underwater plants and animals can be seen easily. Like the Dice in their tunnels."

"I have never seen water animals," said Snore. "There was a stream near the old sett at home, but it was very dark."

"The new water animals prefer polluted water, so long as it is not too bad, and move without walking most of the time. They swim and hunt for food in the water itself. Some of the insects have tiny legs, as many as six or eight."

"Eight legs!" cried Snore.

"Not so loud!" Old Man glanced across the pit. "The Boxes may hear us and stay below ground."

"Sorry!"

"The Water Bottles have six legs. The biggest species is the Great Water Bottle. This is a sketch of one.

"They take deep breaths of air on the surface of the water before swimming down to feed on decayed plants or refuse. To sink, they fill up with water. When they can no longer hold their breath, they squirt it all out and rush up to the air again. That is why we call them Water Bottles."

Snore looked through the sketches of the strange water animals.

"Six legs..." he muttered.

"There's no hurry, but I think it's time we moved closer to the Box earths, Snore." Old Man stood up, keeping as still as possible. "Bring the book with you."

They walked very slowly and sat down by a bush

near the top of the pit, overlooking the entrances.

"So you see, Snore, you have little to fear from the animals in the wood. Just keep out of the way of the big ones. If we get separated, I will wait at the Cottage for you. It is not difficult to find."

Snore looked up from the sketchbook and gazed at the black trees all round the clearing. He thought of the Kite and the Scowl, of the wood at night and how hungry he had felt. Of the furious Syringes and how they had chased him. He looked at Old Man.

"Thank you for helping me," he said simply.

"We are down-wind from the entrances," whispered Old Man. "Go to sleep if you like. I will wake you at dusk or when an animal appears."

Snore fell asleep almost at once. An hour later he was aware of a gentle push. His eyes opened and fixed on a long nose in one of the entrances further down the slope of the pit.

The Box slowly emerged. It looked in all directions,

but did not notice the watchers.

Don't like the look of you. Sharp, pointed head, long legs. Glad Old Man is next to me!

The Box walked with a stiff, rather clumsy gait up the bank, but paused near the top. It stared round the pit again and its angular face, arising from its body without any apparent neck, looked fierce and aggressive. Snore shivered.

As the Box continued over the edge of the pit, its thick white-tipped tail stood out clearly in the fading light. The body was hidden against the sky above and then the white-tip was gone, too.

"Did you see him all right?" Old Man asked and Snore nodded. "He went off rather quickly, I'm afraid, but we may be lucky later."

"He looked like a bully!" said Snore. He felt stiff and stretched quietly.

Half an hour passed. Old Man yawned several times.

"We may have whispered too much. The others could have heard us. Mind you, he might be the only Box living here at present."

Snore rubbed his leg. It tingled from being still for so long. Minutes passed. He became restless again.

I wonder what the tunnel of the old sett is like. Old Man must be too big to go down one. Perhaps he would like me to see for him.

Snore turned to Old Man.

He was fast asleep against the bush and began to

breathe heavily. Snore looked back at the earths and then at Old Man.

I wonder...

He ran down the slope to the nearest entrance. For a moment he sniffed at the hole.

No fresh smell of Boxes, but I'd better be careful. At least Old Man is not far away.

He stepped cautiously into the dark tunnel.

Chapter 10
Night life

At nightfall the Mysterious Greatwood came alive. Over the trees drifted the ghostly shapes of Scowls. They kept to themselves and if a rival came close to their favourite trees, they screeched angrily and gave chase.

Whilst the Scowls beat up and down the paths, Boxes searched through the darkest parts of the wood. A pack of six hunted along one track, but others kept on their own. Occasionally they would meet a herd of Steer browsing by the clearing. They always ignored each other and kept well apart.

The Kites stopped hunting at sunset. There were several pairs and each had a nest of small branches on top of a tall Pinelon. They settled down noisily on their nests, bickering with themselves until after dark.

Busy tapping sounds came from under the trees. The Marbles at work. They glowed brightly in the darkness and seemed to leave little trails of light as they bounced through the air. So, too, did the Mats. Their circular wings sparkled as they left their hiding places in the trees.

Some were as small as the Marbles, others similar in size to the Tin Openers, now safely hidden away in the tree trunks. They all had a carefree, buoyant flight.

Hats, black with short wings, would chase after them, squeaking with excitement and snapping at the colourful wings. They, in turn, took care to avoid the

Scowls and would twist rapidly away through the branches if the familiar white shape of one appeared.

A scream, but no echo. A Box had killed a Robot. Then the pack of six caught another soon after. They greedily fought over the remains and set off to look for more. Some stalked the Dice and would pounce suddenly on to the little square bodies as they came out of cover on the edges of the paths.

To the east, the motorway blazed with yellow lights. Faces of people in cars and lorries would sometimes turn from the road and stare towards the wood. They looked pale and empty in the yellow light. Below them, the black wood kept its sounds and colours to itself. Hidden amongst the trees, the animals hunted or died, or both, unseen.

Chapter 11
Tunnel trails

Snore was nervous at first, but his curiosity overcame his fear. The well worn path went deeper, with dark tunnels leading off here and there.

I do like tunnels! Still no sign of Boxes.

Down, round, up a little, down again. Dampness. No smell of Badgers.

The tunnel ended abruptly in a wide sleeping chamber.

He must live here. Yes, still warm.

Snore was about to turn back and explore other passages when he heard a hiccup. There was another and then two more. He pressed his ear against the wall.

"Hic-hic-hiccup!"

The tunnels must go deeper.

One more hiccup, more distant than the last one and then silence. Snore began to dig deeply into the earth with his strong claws, throwing the soil back behind him.

I wonder why I don't do this more often?

It was not long before a gap appeared in the wall and then the earth fell away to reveal a huge chamber, many times bigger than the tunnel. Snore squeezed through the gap. Before him stood rows of tables covered with plant pots of all sizes. Bushes and small trees grew from them up into the dark roof of the chamber.

Real plants! Real trees!

"Hiccup!"

Snore jumped at the sound. He hid behind the nearest table. An animal came past carrying a large potted tree. It was not like the Box he had seen earlier.

"Hic-hic-hic-Hiccup!"

It was the loudest hiccup that Snore had ever heard and the pot fell from the animal's grasp. There was a crash of breaking pottery and soil spilled across the floor. The animal was so upset that it jumped up and down grumbling and hiccuping furiously.

"Hello," said Snore.

The animal was in mid-jump. It sat down with a gasp and fell backwards over the uprooted tree.

"Who are you?"

"I'm Snore. Everybody calls me Snore, too. I came to see where the Boxes lived. I'm afraid I knocked your wall down to see who was hiccuping."

"Oh," said the animal as it got to its feet. "I thought there were no more Badgers in the wood."

"You know what a Badger looks like!" exclaimed Snore.

"Well, I should do. I happen to be one myself, believe it or not."

"Oh, I am sorry. Your face has got a little muddy. But this is wonderful! I have found you at last! Has Snap found you too?"

"Snap? No, I don't know any Badger called Snap. I'm Nellie, by the way."

"Hello, Nellie."

"Hello. Now then. Let's see. You had better come to meet the others. Oh, dear," she scratched her cheek anxiously. "We've never had anyone knock a hole in our wall before. Wait... Yes! My hiccups have gone! You gave me such a shock, I forgot to do one. I've tried so many ways. I once tried to drink water backwards,

but it ran all down me frontwards. Still, come on!"

Nellie led the way past the tables to a tunnel in the wall.

"It looks very dark for plants to grow," said Snore.

"Hah! That's the problem. I have to carry all the

plants and trees up to a shallow chamber above this one. There are gaps in the roof and during daylight I push the trees and shrubs through the gaps into the sunlight. They are hidden from view amongst the trees.

"I have to bring everything back each evening, otherwise the animals above eat them. There are fewer creatures about in the daytime. Still, it won't be long now..."

Snore was confused by what Nellie said, but they walked into a narrow passage and it was difficult to ask more. They came to several more large rooms, but did not stop.

Nellie finally stopped at a door sunk into the wall. She knocked and a face appeared.

"Hello, Willie. I've brought a visitor to meet Boss Badger."

Willie was much smaller than Snore. He said nothing, but looked curiously at the young Badger. They walked to a narrow room and another animal, just like Willie, appeared from the darkness.

"Sit down."

There was a seat dug out of the wall.

"Who is Willie, Nellie?"

"Willie is a Weasel and guards the tunnel with his brother Wally. They see that nobody dangerous comes to see Boss Badger. Mind you, he's as strong as anything and can easily look after himself."

The Weasel returned and took them into a room. A

voice seemed to boom out:

"I thought I knew all the animals underground, but you are certainly new to me."

It was a Very Big Badger.

Snore smiled nervously.

"I have only just arrived. I ran down a Box earth and knocked down a wall when I heard Nellie hiccup."

"He made me jump," added Nellie. "It stopped my hiccups!"

"Welcome, young friend..."

"Snore," interrupted Nellie.

"Welcome, Snore. We will have to mend the hole in the wall, or all kinds of animals will find us. We have to keep out those living in the wood above. For a little longer, anyway."

"I must go back soon and tell my friend I have found you," said Snore.

"Who is your friend?" asked Boss Badger.

"Old Man."

"Man!" Boss Badger gave a loud snort.

Oh dear. I've said the wrong thing.

"Yes, Old Man," repeated Snore. "But he is very kind. I'm sure he would help us. He saved me from a Kite and helped me look for you. He is writing a book about the animals here and has Dice in his cottage so that he can watch them easily."

Boss Badger frowned and scratched his chin thoughtfully. Nellie tried to ignore the fact that "Man"

had been mentioned. She hummed a little tune to herself and drew patterns on the soil with her foot.

"This evening," Snore continued, "we were watching a Box and I came down to see where it lived in the old sett. I hope Old Man does not think I ran away. He is very friendly."

"You are safer down here, Snore. We never go above ground. We all lived in the wood until the other animals and trees began to take over. After that the wood changed so much that we now have to live underground.

"Old Man must be different from other men. Most men are anything but kind. You are too young to know what the old countryside was like. We had wonderful paths and trails round here. Then people came with concrete and rubbish. They do not come into the wood now, but you have seen for yourself what happened."

Far above ground, Old Man was walking round the clearing.

"Snore! Snore! Where are you?"

He shouted into each earth. There was no reply. No sound from below.

He finally sat down and shook his head. It seemed obvious. Snore had found the earths too attractive. He wanted to live underground again.

"I hope the Boxes do not harm you, my friend."

He stood up and climbed the pit edge. A glance back towards the earths, nearly hidden in the darkness. No little black and white face. He turned away and walked sadly towards the trees and his cottage.

Chapter 12
An Otter's pool

"How did the new animals drive you all underground?" Snore asked Boss Badger.

"The new animals took over the wood and as their trees spread, we had to keep in a smaller and smaller area. We believe in live and let live. They are not content with the rubbish tips, but just take over everything. We were not united at first, but as things got worse we rescued what we could of the old trees and plants and brought them down here. The rest have probably been destroyed in the wood by now. All kinds of animals joined us here and we made the tunnels and rooms much larger. The rest, insects, reptiles and so on manage as best they can round mountains and the older sort of gardens."

"We have a major battle ahead when we go above ground to win back the wood and we will have to plant our own trees when we return. I'm glad to say that Nellie looks after them very well."

Nellie smiled and gave a little hiccup.

"People don't like the new wood at all. They don't know we are still here, otherwise they would have dug us out long ago. They hunted the Boxes on little motor bicycles for a time, but soon became bored with that."

"You must be hungry, Snore," said Nellie. "I will get us all something to eat."

Boss Badger and Snore sat amongst the grassy bedding in the chamber. Nellie returned. "This is very tasty!" said Snore.

"It is a mixture of mushrooms and insect larvae. Tell me how you came to the wood."

Snore explained between mouthfuls of food. Boss Badger listened carefully.

Finally he sat back and looked thoughtfully at the ground. Nellie smiled at Snore and put her paw to her mouth, as if to say "Shh!"

After a few minutes, Boss Badger turned to them.

"Nellie, would you like to show Snore our underground home? I have some planning to do."

Nellie led Snore past Wally and Willie to a wide section of tunnels.

"I will show you our main tunnels, where most of the animals live. You can meet some of them if you like."

"What do you think Boss Badger will do?" asked Snore.

"I don't know. He makes up his own mind. That's how it should be. He is our leader."

"Is he a good leader?"

"Oh yes. We all love him. He is very brave."

Nellie pointed at the tunnel entrances that led from the main path, "Stoats live down there, Pine Martens there, Moles, Squirrels..."

"It's huge!"

"Not big enough for most of the animals! We feel very overcrowded at times. There are so many of us. Would you like to see the Holt, where the Otters live?"

"Yes please."

"It's right at the end of the tunnel. Not really a Holt, but they are close to the old river and have a pond there."

A Vole appeared and hurried past with a brief "Good evening."

"Where is everyone?" asked Snore. "I should have thought the tunnels would fill up in the evening."

"They usually do, but everyone is working on the stores of sticks and mud pies. We used to find that they frightened off the new animals best of all. You wouldn't

believe how nasty they were to us."

They passed a Hedgehog curled up on the side of the tunnel. He was grumbling to himself. Nellie stopped.

"What's the matter, Henry? This is no place to sit."

Henry took no notice and continued to grumble.

"Is he all right?" asked Snore.

"Oh yes," said Nellie. They walked on. "He finds life in these crowded tunnels too confusing. I heard that he often sits in the tunnels and mopes. The sooner we get back above ground the better."

The air became misty towards the end.

"The passages seem endless!" laughed Snore.

"Nearly there! Think of all the other smaller tunnels down here, too. This must be the biggest Badger sett ever. Not that we call it that anymore. It is a home for all animals now."

"Aren't there any Birds down here?"

"No. We used to see them occasionally before all was closed up. The rare ones still live in the mountains of the north country, so I hear. They say that Butterflies have been seen round the houses in summer, too."

"Snap said he saw one. We saw a Wasp and a Blackbird in some of the old gardens."

A large side tunnel loomed out of the mist.

"Here we are."

Nellie led Snore along a damp passage to a door. There were sounds of splashing and loud whistles as they entered.

Through the mist Snore could see a long pool of water. Otters seemed to be everywhere, swimming, jumping and diving. A long mud slide led into the pool at the far end. One after another, Otters slid into the water, whistling with joy to each other.

"They are so playful," said Nellie. "No boredom in this part of our home!" She dropped her voice. "They probably suffered more than any animal at the hand of Man."

Snore waved to the animals and was showered with water in return. There were cheerful sounds of chattering and an Otter clambered out of the pool to join them.

"This is Snore, Oswald."

Snore shook a wet paw.

"Sorry to soak you, Snore! We've just finished making mud pies."

"I need a wash!"

"Come outside. It's always noisy in here."

Nellie explained how Snore had come to the wood and Oswald led them through the main tunnel to the river.

The bank hid the surface from view. It hung over the end of the tunnel in a wide screen.

"Are we still under the wood?" asked Snore.

"Yes," replied Oswald. "The river comes through to the north of the clearing."

"Where you came into the Badger sett," added Nellie. "Do you swim in there as well?"

"Only a little way. The water is fresh now and the fish are coming back, but we dare not go far. If men saw us they might hunt us out and find the underground tunnel. It may be safe, but we dare not risk it in case we spoil the return of all the animals to the wood. We threw away most of the soil dug out of the extra tunnels into the water here. So that nobody would see."

They stood for a moment, looking down into the flowing water.

Lovely, relaxing water. I would like to be an Otter. Just for a little while anyway.

"I think we should go back," said Nellie. "Boss Badger will wonder where we are."

They made their way to the main tunnel.

"See you later, Oswald!"

"And you, Snore!"

Into the mist. A farewell wave.

Chapter 13
Fighting back

When Nellie and Snore returned, Boss Badger was still seated, deep in thought. He jumped up.

"The time has come for action, Snore!" He strode swiftly to the entrance to his room.

"Wally!"

Wally looked very sleepy.

"Yes, Boss Badger?"

"We are going to go above ground. Please bring all the animal leaders here as soon as possible. Your long vigil outside my door will soon be a thing of the past!"

"I've never seen him quite like this before," whispered Nellie to Snore.

A stream of animals came to the room. There was a buzz of excited conversation. Several leaders for each kind of animal had come, all eager to hear the news.

Oswald waved and spoke to a Fox. Faces turned to Snore as word went round that a newcomer had arrived. Boss Badger stood on a large flint and raised an arm. All talking ceased.

"My fellows. The time has come for action. At the last meeting we decided to prepare to go above ground. We discussed all the difficulties and these may still apply, but we have a young Badger, Snore, who not only walked safely through the wood, but made friends

with a man!"

All eyes fixed on Snore and excited chatter broke out.

Could it be true that a Badger had made friends with a man?

Snore tried to look at Boss Badger, and pretended not to notice.

"My fellows," continued Boss Badger, "we must gather our stores and be prepared to fight to take back what is rightfully ours. If we stick together, we will win. I look forward to the day when our Squirrels can live in real trees, trees which grow leaves and produce real wood.

"All those who agree that we go tonight say 'Yes'."

"YES!"

"Those who think we should wait, say 'No'."

No sound. Then a weak "No" came from one corner of the room. A Stoat shouted:

"It's all right. It's only Nervous Norman. He said 'Yes' the first time, anyway!"

Norman, a timid Pygmy Shrew, who had only become a leader because he was the least frightened of all the Pygmy Shrews, said he was sorry and tried to hide behind the nearest chair.

"Then we are all agreed!" cried Boss Badger. "Get everyone together. I will meet you all at the North tunnel door. When we are above ground use the sticks to defend yourselves!"

Is this really happening? It seems as if I'm in a

dream.

"We will try to have a circle of animals round the earths by daybreak. Bring along all the mud pies and sticks you can manage. We have large reserves, I know, but they will soon run down. Once we have part of the wood to ourselves, we can start to grow our real trees and plants again."

There were shouts of joy. Boss Badger stood down and the animals rushed out. Willie and Wally stood either side of the door and cheered them on their way.

"See what we have started, Snore!"

Snore just stared.

"Rest here for a while. Nellie and I will be busy with preparations."

Snore curled up and watched Boss Badger and Nellie sorting out maps.

Chapter 14
A new dawn

"Wake Up!"

It was Wally. Willie and Nellie were close by and they smiled at Snore.

"We're off to the pit where you came in, Snore!" said Nellie.

All kinds of animals joined them as they passed through tunnel after tunnel. Ahead stood Boss Badger.

"Looks as though we're going to use the official exit," said Nellie, "not your hole in the wall!"

Boss Badger raised his arms.

"Remember to keep in a circle. We will be troubled by the brightness of the daylight in the morning, but if we stand our ground, we can begin to plant round the pit." Boss Badger marched forward. Snore followed close behind, with Nellie and the two Weasels.

Fresh air mingled with the close underground atmosphere. An entrance loomed ahead, speckled with stars in the sky above the wood.

Boss Badger stopped. He edged forward to sniff the clear night air.

"All seems quiet."

The animals, clutching sticks and mud pies, climbed cautiously from the entrance and stood in groups in the bottom of the pit. There was an air of intense excitement, but all were silent.

Boss Badger whispered to Snore.

"Look for Old Man or any animals round the top of the pit. Be very careful."

Snore crawled quietly up the side of the pit.

Slowly, now. Ah, this is the same pit. Old Man was by that bush.

He reached the top of the pit and looked towards the black trees.

Nothing there. Slowly round, no, nothing. Nor over there, wait.

Something was in the clearing. Snore quietly raised and lowered his arm to Boss Badger and the black forms below seemed to crumple on to the ground. The animals lay close to each other, ears alert for the slightest sound.

It's stopped moving, no there it is, further over. Fairly small.

Snore peered round the dark clearing, then back at the shape. It was approaching but moving slowly towards the other side of the pit. Snore lowered his head and edged along to meet the shape. He felt the hairs on his back stiffen as he raised his black and white nose. The shape had gone. Snore looked in all directions. Nothing. He sniffed deeply and his hairs relaxed.

There's no scent. The wind's wrong anyway. How odd. It was here a moment ago.

He stood and looked round.

"Keep down!" hissed Boss Badger from below. It was too late. A black form sprung from the ground.

Snore had no time to turn. With a sudden jolt, the line of black trees spun sideways and over. He was falling. Claws dug into his back and the pit edge knocked the air from his chest.

Snore had one defence. He was able to turn his head back and up into the neck of the creature. He bit hard.

"Snore!"

"Snap!"

Boss Badger wrenched away the top animal.

"It's all right!" Snore spat out a mouthful of hairs. "It's my brother!"

"What a welcome!" growled Snap, but even in the dark Snore could see a brief smile cross his face.

"I thought I would never see you again! This is Boss Badger. He is the leader of all these animals. This is Snap, Boss Badger."

"Glad you found us! We need all the help we can get..."

"Box!"

It was a Hare. He ran down to Boss Badger.

"A Box is coming towards the pit!"

They turned as the Box arrived above the sett. It circled round and then retreated.

"Every Box in the wood will know about us now," said Boss Badger. "Still, we have to face them sooner or later."

At the top of the pit, the animals spread out into a circle and advanced towards the trees. All was quiet.

"Tell me later how you got here," whispered Snore to Snap. He nodded.

Near the edge of the clearing, they stopped and began to build small camps with any sticks or debris they could find. Boss Badger kept walking round the circle, making sure that all was well.

"Our main strength lies in our Badgers, Foxes and Otters," said Nellie. "There are about ten of each. You must meet the others later."

"We ought to spread out amongst the smaller animals. Let's go with that Mole over there," said Snore.

Digby Mole smiled as Snore approached.

"You will have Snap on one side and me on the other!"

"Good! Can't wait to get my claws into a Box or two!"

"HELP!"

Across the clearing, a large Steer was trying to throw off three Rabbits. They clung to its back and antlers.

"HELP!" one cried again. The Steer saw the Badgers and tossed back its head. A doe Rabbit was flung into the air. The others fell off and the Steer ran away into the trees.

"Well done, Rabbits!" shouted Snore.

The Rabbit thrown from the antlers looked rather sorry for herself. She rubbed her head and could only

muster a rather weak smile for her friends.

Boss Badger appeared, congratulated the Rabbits and organised the animals back into line.

"The Steer live in herds," Snore explained to Snap.

"The old ones were very friendly," said Digby, "but these new ones drove them off. I did hear that some were still living in old gardens near the border of the wood."

Before long there was a faint light in the eastern sky. Snore looked up. They had cleared a patch under a Pinelon on the edge of the clearing and each was mixing mud pies.

Dawn. It will be light soon.

He looked round.

Snap on one side and all these wonderful animals round about. The Badgers at last!

Chapter 15
Mole warfare

Snap was scratching his back noisily. It was morning and Snore blinked in the sunlight.

"I wish something would happen, Snap!"

Snap stopped scratching and looked up.

"Better to sit in the sun than fight!" he shouted back.

Snore yawned. He walked over and sat down.

"I must say it makes a change to sit down all morning! Now then. Tell me what happened to you, after the van went off."

"You were lucky, as always!" said Snap.

Snore grinned.

"Did you make the van stop again?"

"No. It went on up the motorway and didn't come to a halt until we were in a big store-house."

"What did you do ?"

"I jumped, of course. The man came after me, but I hid amongst tins and boxes. The building was full of them. Other men arrived, but they couldn't find me. Then night came and I had a good feed up!"

"Hm!" said Snore. "I was starving then! The wood is hopeless for food."

"Next day," continued Snap, "they came and put down some traps, silly lot! During the morning the van came back and I thought it was time to get away. It was difficult, but I jumped down on to the back again as it left."

"Did it come back past the wood?"

"Yes! Just as I had hoped. But the driver still wouldn't stop. I got desperate. He had a load of empty crates this time. They were smaller than those apple ones we came up on and I started to push them off the back. You should have seen the cars behind! I got three over the side and then the driver realised what was happening."

"Well done!"

"It wasn't as simple as all that," said Snap. "The wood was on the other side of the motorway."

"Of course."

"I got across to the centre all right. The traffic had stopped when the crates fell in front of them, but the road was just as busy on the other side. I ran across and just missed a lorry. The van driver was after me. I couldn't wait."

"Did you find my trail?"

"Yes. I walked along the edge of the wood and eventually saw your pad marks in a soft patch under the trees. I hurried because it was getting late. At dusk I got to the clearing and scented Man as well. At the sett I thought you were something eatable!"

"That was obvious!" laughed Snore.

"Well, you looked peculiar half hidden by the pit. I was so hungry I jumped as soon as you stood up."

"Nellie gave you some food, didn't she?"

"Yes. She had some with her. Delicious. Now, tell me what happened to you."

They sat, enjoying the sunshine. Snore became restless.

He went over to see Digby, but there was no sign of him. Then Snore saw Marbles bouncing round fresh heaps of soil.

"Digby! What are you doing?"

Digby was in the bottom of a Marble hill. He was surrounded by Marbles and was singing a little song as he worked.

"Hello, Snore! Come and join me! This is great fun.

Marbles, Marbles, everywhere..."

"Why are you digging up the Marbles?"

"Got bored. Anyway, can't have these little animals round our pit...There she is!"

He plunged down and lifted a huge yellow Marble out of the soil.

"The Queen, Snore, look!"

She lay quietly in his wide paws, but the rest of the colony was in a frenzy. Digby ran off into the wood, followed by a long column of hysterical Marbles. The nest emptied. A few stragglers bounced about but quickly found the trail and were gone.

"What's happening here?"

It was Boss Badger.

"Hello. Digby dug out a Marble hill and has just run off into the trees with the Queen. Here he is now."

Digby ran up, wiping his claws on his chest.

"Well done, Digby, but try to keep in line."

"I thought I ought to move the nest. They will dig another in the wood," said Digby. "I'll get on with my missile launcher."

"Good idea. I'm sorry about all this waiting, but we can't begin to bring trees above ground at this stage."

Snore went back to his place and Boss Badger continued his round.

"Let's climb this tree, Snap."

"Why? The old Badger wants us to keep in line."

"I could keep a look-out. See if any animals are

approaching," said Snore.

"Do as you like. I'm staying here," said Snap, and he began to mould another mud pie.

The Pinelon branches dipped close to the ground. Snore swung quickly up to the trunk. It was easier to climb there.

I may get a good view. The Pinelons are taller than the other trees.

He pushed through long black strands and, near the top, peered out over the dark trees. The wood spread out all round. Behind and below was the clearing with its circle of animals, restless in the sunlight. A few paths cut through the trees, but there was no sign of life.

What's that? Ah, Kite. Long way away, though. What a wood. Can we ever win back all this?

A movement below. There's something down on that path. Yes. There. Two, three... Boxes! Lots of them!

Snore scrambled down the tree, shouting. Boss Badger ran up.

"We're ready for them, Snore. Can you be responsible for the mud pie missile launcher? I hope it will work. Digby gets these ideas... you know, very good and all that, but he's liable to fire them all off before the Boxes have left cover."

Snore looked in vain for Digby, but found the curious missile launcher by the trees.

"Up here, Snore!"

Mole warfare

Snore looked up.

Digby waved from the branches above the launcher.

"Come down, Digby! The Boxes are coming!"

"Essential to be up here, old boy."

"Why?"

"To launch the mud pies, like so..."

"Stop!" cried Snore.

Digby was about to jump on to the long stick which was set to throw the pies into the air.

"I'll tell you when to jump. Try to keep silent for now."

Word of the Boxes had circulated the pit area. The animals lay out of sight in their small camps and waited.

All was quiet. Waiting, waiting.

The Boxes assembled under the trees on the border of the clearing. Their fiery yellow eyes stared out at the circle of animals. Unable to see them clearly, the Boxes repeatedly sniffed the air.

Snore trembled with excitement.

Five, six, seven pairs of eyes. Seven. No, more over there, eight, nine, ten. I hope we can hold them.

The line of Boxes advanced silently into the open. Their heads hung low and their pace quickened. The leading animal howled. Heads down, eyes blazing, the Boxes ran at the line.

Boss Badger stood up.

"At them!"

A hail of mud pies flew into the air and on to the
Boxes. Several Shrews threw pies in the wrong
direction but the general effect was stunning. The
Boxes stopped in their tracks and then fled back to the
wood, dripping with mud. More mud pies thumped to
the ground round them.

"Keep in line!" shouted Boss Badger.

Snore smiled across at Snap, but he was still looking
anxiously after the Boxes. Snore followed his line of

sight and tensed. A sinister row of antlers appeared by the far line of trees.

"You didn't tell me to jump!"

It was Digby.

"I'll tell you when!"

Oh dear, I forgot! Better pretend it was good tactics. Perhaps it was, this looks dangerous.

"This time, when I give the word, Digby."

One after another, the Steer led across the clearing and joined the Boxes.

Thirty! They're joining up. No wonder the Boxes look pleased.

A line formed and started towards the circle.

"Sticks this time!" cried Boss Badger.

It was more frightening than before. There was now the thunder of hooves and vibrations shook the ground. Antlers swung down and forward. Air hissed noisily in and out of their heaving lungs.

"Keep calm! Everything you've got!"

The sticks hurt. The Boxes stopped altogether but the Steer only slowed down. Some paused, then ran on.

"Jump!" yelled Snore.

Digby giggled and leapt into space. He was so excited he missed the launcher and vanished into the empty Marble hill.

Snore looked across at the centre of the fighting. The line had held, but a Steer had avoided two Otters and was trying to get past Snap. Snore threw a large stick with all his strength and this wedged between the antlers, across its eyes. With confused vision it ran into the trees and became entangled in the dense lower branches.

"Watch out, Snore!"

Digby had climbed the tree again.

"Wait! They are too close to our line..." Snore was too late.

Digby landed firmly on the stick this time. It bent in an arc and shot the platform with rows of pies upwards. The 'woosh!' noise of the pies in the air had an immediate effect. It sounded like an attack by hawks from above. The Steer and Boxes stopped fighting and turned for cover.

Digby just had time to sit up and exclaim: "Magnificent!" when the platform landed on his head. He sank back, unconscious, but smiling.

The pies rained down on the fleeing enemy. In no time the clearing was empty and there was only the sound of distant howling from terrified Boxes.

"Good thing they didn't know we only had one of those," observed Snap.

"You Otters and Badgers after them!" shouted Boss Badger.

Snore ran across the clearing shouting and waving the long stick from the missile launcher. Oswald Otter was ahead. When they came to the trees again, they trailed the Boxes and Steer along the main path. Snore

recognised it as the one he had followed when he came into the wood.

"We've got them on the run, now!" laughed Oswald.

The shouts from behind sent the Boxes out of the wood and along the edge of the motorway. The Steer streamed in a line up the bank and a car had to swerve to avoid the first one. Behind, a lorry mounted the verge and turned across the carriageway. The driver jumped out and ran along the roadside to an alarm point. All traffic had stopped or was stopping on the automatic safety halt system under the road surface.

"Animals! All over the place."

"The wood's overflowing with them!"

"Down there! Them Wolf things."

A great, unreasoning fear swept through people in the lines of cars and lorries. There were screams of hysteria as the shout of "Wolf!" went down the motorway. Windows closed and doors were locked. People desperately tried to get clear of the safety halt system and drive their vehicles away, crashing into each other in their haste to escape animals they thought belonged to the past.

Snore and Oswald stopped at the edge of the wood and watched the confusion. Boss Badger arrived, out of breath from the chase.

"They were really frightened. It doesn't look as if they'll return in a hurry."

"We must get Digby to build lots of his missile launchers round the pit!" laughed Snore.

Chapter 16
The fire

"Burn the place down!" came the shout. A line of cars had drawn up by the wood. It was dusk and the men nervously flashed torches out of the windows towards the black trees.

"What if we're caught?"

"Nobody lives on this side. It's deserted. They'll never do anything about this place unless we do."

"I'm not so sure now. After all, it was the last wood of any size."

"The animals have reached pest proportions. You saw for yourself. There are enough round the houses, but at this rate we'll be completely overrun."

"What about the motorway on the far side?"

"There's a fire break. It wouldn't reach the road."

"I'm still not sure. Nobody likes wolves, but there are so many animals in there. We could insist that the wood is sprayed. I'd prefer that to fire."

"No, sprays are no good. A good fire is the only answer, or we'll have the same trouble in a few years."

A door opened and one of the men threw a plastic Flami-rod into the air. Then another. The explosions sent a huge wall of flames bursting into the trees. The wood was lit by a blinding flash and tree after tree was engulfed.

"Look at the colours!"

"I'm sure there is a more humane way..."

The fire spread rapidly into the wood

"Never seen a fire burn so quickly."

"Best thing. Nobody went there. Horrid place."

"Those poor animals. The old forest fires must have been like this."

"No, the old trees didn't burn so fast."

"I'm off, or the Foam Lorries will arrive and catch us here."

The animals living amongst the trees knew nothing of flames and made no attempt to escape. Smoke swirled round them in their retreats or as they flew. They dropped into a confused sleep and fell over without a sound. None could overcome the gas in the smoke.

It had no scent, caused no pain, but swirled above the ground in a deadly, invisible mist. The fire consumed all in its path.

Snore ran to the edge of the pit.

"Look at those lights above the wood!"

"And listen to the noise," said Snap.

Boss Badger joined them.

"Looks like trouble. Is anyone outside the pit?"

"No," answered Snore. "When Digby came-to and felt all right we took him below. We were the last out there."

"It's coming closer," said Snap. He sneezed as a thin wisp of smoke drifted across the clearing and round the pit.

"Everyone underground!" cried Boss Badger. "I won't post guards round the clearing after all."

Many had already gone down to sleep in their tunnels.

"Wait," said Snore. "Old Man said he lived over there. He promised to wait for me at his cottage if ever we were separated."

"He'll be able to look after himself," replied Boss Badger. "It's too dangerous to go now. Where's Snap?"

They were about to close the heavy exit door. Snore went back to the surface.

"Snap! What are you doing?"

Snap looked puzzled, unwell.

"The... smoke..." He fell to the ground with a sigh.

Snore pulled him quickly to the tunnel.

"He's not feeling well."

"We all need a long sleep," said Boss Badger and they made their way below, carrying Snap.

Nellie appeared.

"I've filled in that hole you made in the wall, Snore! What are you holding? Oh dear, is Snap all right?"

The cottage stood just outside the wood. The road to it had long been overgrown and few people knew it was still there.

Old Man was asleep. He had fed the animals and gone straight to bed. In his deep sleep, he did not notice the roar of burning trees.

The smoke came first. It penetrated the old window frames and slowly filled the cottage with its deadly fumes. Old Man coughed quietly in his sleep.

"I do feel... strange..." he muttered out loud.

Suddenly he was awake. He leapt out of bed and ran to the window. As he did so, the glass shattered in the heat. He stumbled back, confused and still sleepy. All around seemed to be blazing. Hideous colours... heat... smoke...

"The animals!"

Old Man's brain cleared. He ran to the stairs but they were already on fire. He began to choke. The air was full of dense smoke.

The front windows!

He ran across the landing. The windows were still intact and he flung them wide, clung for a moment to the window sill and then dropped on to the garden below. As he jumped, the upstairs floor fell into the flames and the old wooden roof began to crackle as fire flickered up the beams and under the tiles.

Old Man ran down the path, gasping for air. He felt his whiskers smouldering in the intense heat and covered his face with his hands.

The wall of fire spread in brilliant colours and with a constant, thunderous noise towards the clearing, leaving black emptiness in its wake.

Its speed amazed onlookers. Several airborne craft approached and poured foam in a line round the fire area. Without air, the flames died down almost as quickly as they had started.

On the ground, Hover-Wagons left wide channels of foam, but they were not necessary. By midnight, the fire was out and the wood gone. People who had driven to watch the flames went home and the only house affected was Old Man's cottage.

Chapter 17
Lost records

Digby left his elaborate drawings and plans for a defence network and went to look round Boss Badger's large door.

"The heat has died down. Even by the exit door."

"Good! Thank you, Digby."

Snore and Nellie were with Boss Badger. He turned to them.

"Let's go and see what happened. Is Snap all right?"

"Much better," said Snore. "Bit of a headache now, that's all. I'll see if he wants to come up with us."

Digby ran off to tell the animal leaders the news.

The exit boulders were black, with deep scorch marks. Boss Badger looked carefully out of the tunnel entrance. Followed by Snore, Snap and Nellie, he climbed to the top of the charred pit.

Snap sniffed the air suspiciously.

"Hm! Bit better this morning." His head throbbed as he spoke and he fell silent with a pained grunt.

It was an incredible sight. On the east side of the clearing, in a long, undulating panorama were blackened stumps where each tree once stood. The Pinelons had melted into large mis-shapen lumps and the clearing was covered in a soft black powder.

Snore broke the silence.

"I must find Old Man. I wish he'd shown me where his cottage stood."

"It must be the one over in that direction," said Boss Badger. "There were no others actually on the edge of the wood." He looked back at the sett and thought for a moment. "Yes, over there. It's difficult to get bearings now. Do you want any help?"

Snore shook his head. He ran off along the traces of a path.

Poor Old Man, poor Old Man.

Snore felt anxious, upset. So much had happened in a short time. Every so often he stopped and peered ahead to see if the cottage was in view. The featureless ground receded into the distance.

Just thousands of blobs. It's amazing. All in one night.

He kept to the dusty trail. It was still hot in places.

I wonder if the cottage would burn.

At the top of a slight incline, Snore spotted a shape larger than the molten Pinelons or burnt stumps.

"Old Man!"

He ran, waving and shouting.

As he came closer, he found it was a group of three Pinelons that had sunk into a curious twisted shape in the fire. He ran on and frantic thoughts rushed through his head.

He can't have gone. He can't have gone.

"Old Man! Old Man! Old Man!"

Silence.

Snore set off again and came to heaps of blackened rubble. Old houses and rubbish heaps lined the horizon, marking the original edge of the Mysterious Greatwood.

He stood for a few moments. Then it dawned on him.

The cottage! This must be the cottage!

Lines of bricks marked where the walls had stood. These had collapsed under the weight of fallen trees, and some parts looked as if they were glued to the ground under the Pinelons.

Snore felt desperate. He ran amongst the chaos looking for signs of Old Man.

"Not much left, Snore!"

It was Old Man.

He must have been sitting here in the ruins.

Snore was speechless and felt a surge of joy and relief.

"What a night!" said Old Man. "Where did you get to?"

Snore stared at him.

"I-I was in the sett. There's so much to tell you..."

It was all he could say. They sat down on the warm bricks.

"I hoped you would be safe," said Old Man, slowly. "I only just escaped in time. This is all I have left." He indicated his pyjamas.

Snore still stared at Old Man. His beard looked

smaller and his eyes were dark and strained. There was no sign of his load of oddments.

Old Man scratched the singed hairs on his chin.

"The whole wood seems to have been destroyed. I don't mind the cottage being burnt down so much, but all my animals have gone as well. And those in the wood, of course. I expect some of the Boxes and Steer will still linger round the borders, but there is no cover left for them here. I had no idea these trees burnt so quickly. Or that the Pinelons gave off that gas in the smoke."

They looked round at the still emptiness.

"Those poor animals," whispered Snore, staring sadly

at the black earth.

"They wouldn't have suffered. The chemicals in the smoke would make them unconscious first. This fire spread so quickly, I'm sure there was no pain for them."

Snore suddenly looked up, then around at the ruins of the cottage.

"Your book! Your drawings, traps, everything. Gone!"

Old Man nodded.

He looked into Old Man's face. It was pale and expressionless, but only for a moment. He nodded slowly and sighed.

"It seems to be such a waste. I hate to lose things. It takes so much time to record observations and time is the most precious thing we have. But at least we are alive and well." He winked unexpectedly. "Mustn't grumble!"

Snore felt better. Life had returned to Old Man's face.

"Tell me what happened when you left me in the pit, Snore. I didn't wake up until late yesterday and expected you to turn up at the cottage all day. It seemed best to wait there and I had plenty to do at home."

Chapter 18
A Concrite solution

Black powder hung in the air after each footstep. The clearing came into view. All round the pit stood young trees and it had become a green oasis in the black, scorched earth.

Nellie led a line of animals, some digging, some planting. She fussed round each young stem until she was sure the roots were packed firmly down. Boss Badger was talking to her. He glanced up, saw them and waved. They waved back.

"Come on, Old Man!" Snore pulled at his arm and laughed. "Come and see the new wood!"

"This seems so unreal!" said Old Man.

The animals sat round him in a ring that spread back over the edge of the pit.

"Tell me about the illness which killed the people," said Boss Badger. "We thought the Greatwood was still surrounded and there were just as many people. The new animals were so cruel to us, we didn't have time to notice what was happening outside."

"The Virus, as I told Snore, was more deadly than The Plague, which killed so many people in the past. They think it started in a research centre and what followed must rank as the most devastating coincidence in history. Scientists were studying primates."

"Primates?" asked Snore.

"Monkeys. Big apes, just like me. Anyway, an unknown virus, probably several, got inside the bodies of the humans and they became ill after a meeting in Central Europe, across the sea from here. Scientists had attended from every country in the world. They flew to and from the meeting, so the story goes, in the giant aircraft of the day with hundreds of other travellers. In a few days, thousands of people had unknowingly come into contact with The Virus and taken it home with them. In weeks, every country of the world reported sudden deaths from mystery illnesses. Only a few minor islands escaped what followed.

"I lost my own family and five years later it was estimated that the world population had dropped to a fraction of its former size. In this country, for instance, only about one million people are alive even today. Yet there are buildings, roads and factories to support three hundred million."

"So the concrete, bricks and roads are left all round us with only a few people to live there?"

Old Man nodded.

"Nor will they ever be used as far as I can see. It is rare to find a family with more than two children. The population is now stable, even falling slightly, all over the world.

"I had given up hope for the nature of old, although

fish and other water life are coming back to our seas and rivers at long last. Now Snore has introduced me to all of you. There is suddenly so much to hope for."

"Who set fire to the wood?" asked Snap.

"I don't know," replied Old Man. "It was probably just a few scared people. Snore told me that the Boxes and Steer ran out on to the motorway. There is so much ignorance about animals nowadays that men are easily frightened. At least the fire was put out."

"It will be a long fight to re-grow all of the wood," said Snap, as practical as ever.

"We are not in a hurry, we must just keep together and win every fight," replied Boss Badger. "What will you do now, Old Man?"

He thought for some moments and then smiled.

"Well, may I ask a great favour of you all?"

All the animals joined in. First of all Pinelons were pushed across the top of the pit in rows. Then came smaller trees, layers of branches, soil and grass to keep the rain out with an entrance left on one side big enough for Old Man to crawl inside.

The Badgers dragged in bedding for themselves and for Old Man's new home.

"What will you do about food?" asked Snore.

"That's not going to be difficult," said Old Man. "I know good areas to scavenge for fruits and vegetables. Winters are always a problem, but with careful

planning and storage, all should be well. I managed
alone in the years after The Virus and things were far
worse then. But remember, I am still not a complete
primitive. No ape man ever wore pyjamas!"

Old Man was filling a gap in the roof of the pit
helped by Snore and Digby. Boss Badger appeared at
the entrance, dragging part of a burnt Pinelon.

"All peaceful round the clearing?" asked Old Man.

"Not a sign of life, even round the borders at present.
I was looking at all those empty houses. Is there any
way we could get rid of them?"

"I have been thinking about this for a long time," said
Old Man. "After all, our aim must be to not only re-
grow the old Mysterious Greatwood, but to extend the
trees and fields across the derelict land. There is no
quick answer to the damage of years, although one idea

for rather drastic action did cross my mind."

"What was that?"

Boss Badger sat down.

"There is a type of animal from Africa which eats concrete and bricks..."

"I remember!" interrupted Snore. "The Concrites!"

"Concrites?" muttered Digby.

"All we need do is release them round the houses!" cried Snore.

"Well, yes, Snore," continued Old Man, "but we must remember two very important points. Firstly, we may be unable to get any Concrites. Secondly, if we did and they were released, they would probably get out of control. They used to be kept in the London Zoo research centre, but things might have changed."

"All the Zoo exhibits were animated plastic ones, but the centre had a collection of real animals to study. Nobody was allowed to enter the wooden containers without guards in case a colony of Concrites escaped and consumed London. They spread very quickly and make new colonies all the time, given space and food."

"But it does seem to be the answer to our problem," insisted Snore. "We could keep them in the right places. It wouldn't be like the other new animals that took over the wood. These would only go where they found concrete and bricks."

"I know how you feel, Snore," said Old Man.

"Nothing ventured, nothing gained. We could just find out if they are still kept at the Zoo. It would be wonderful to clear the land so that the old countryside can take the place of the concrete wastes and rubbish dumps."

Digby's eyes brightened. His mind filled with ideas for catapulting Concrites safely into the tops of the tall buildings to eat their way earthwards.

Boss Badger stood up.

"I think we should call a meeting, put the idea to all the animals and see what they think."

Old Man climbed the rough grass bank on to a deserted road. It was dusk and there was a glow of yellow light in the distant sky. Snore, Snap and Digby joined him.

"It is easy to find London at night," said Old Man quietly, pointing at the sky ahead. "I hope the Zoo centre will be as easy to find."

"Look out for stray Boxes and Steer," whispered Snap.

"No sign of them yet," replied Digby and he began to hum to himself.

"It is an amusing thought," said Old Man, "that if we did manage to 'borrow' a colony of Concrites and they ate all the buildings and roads, people who didn't bother to stop them would have to re-build with wood!"

"They would have to start growing trees again,"

laughed Snore.

"Might even let them have a few of ours!" added Digby.

They came to a major roadway which led to the first line of dark buildings.

"Just think," said Old Man, looking up at the high blocks of houses, "we may be at the end of the Concrete Age."

Snap looked serious.

"I'm not so sure. We still have a long, long way to go."

Snore sighed.

"Typical," he said. "Typical!"

And they all laughed.

Projects

You can make models of the characters in *The Mysterious Greatwood* from folded paper or existing materials. Some of the pupils of Cuffley School, (near the original *Great Wood* in Hertfordshire which inspired the story in the 1960s) made those pictured below when their teachers Katie Arnold, Alison Patrick and Kate Wells set a modelling project based on the book.

Katie kindly pictured some of the Dice created in school and sent these to the author with delightful thank-you letters from the children who took part.

The original window display models from the book launch at Hamish Hamilton offices in Great Russell Street, London, are shown opposite: polystyrene Dice and a Marble Eater made from plastic bottles chasing table tennis ball Marbles.

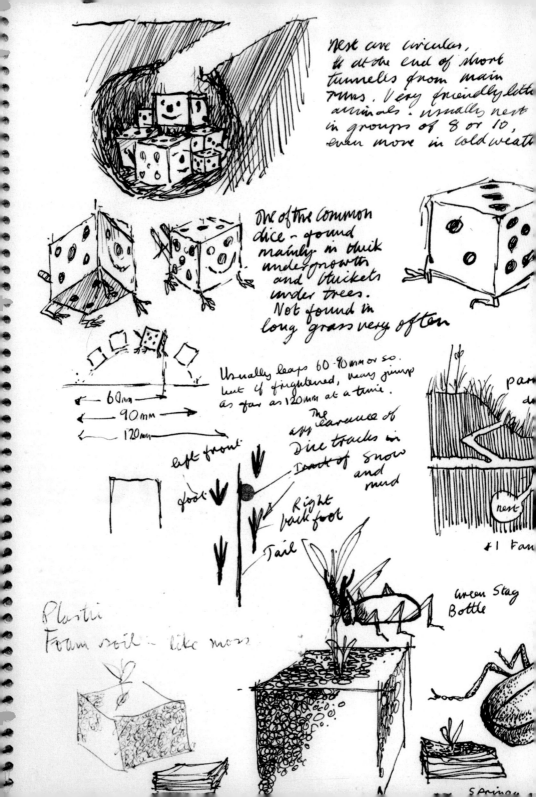

Nest are circular, & at the end of short tunnels from main runs. Very friendly little animals. usually nest in groups of 8 or 10, even more in cold weath...

One of the common dice - found mainly in thick undergrowth and thickets under trees. Not found in long grass very often

60mm
90mm
120mm

Usually leaps 60-90mm or so, but if frightened, may jump as far as 120mm at a time.

left front foot

The appearance of Dice tracks in frost of snow and mud

Right back foot

Tail

par...

nest

#1 Fan...

Green Stag Bottle

Plastic Foam soil - like moss

Spring...